FIVE GOLDEN RINGS

Also by Kimila Kay

STONEYBROOK MYSTERIES

Redneck Ranch (2023)

MEXICO MAYHEM SERIES

Peril in Paradise (2019)

Malice in Mazatlan (2022)

Vanished in Vallarta (2023)

ANTHOLOGIES

"Whispering Willows" Whispers (2023)

"Happy Birthday" Harbinger (2023)

"Table Talk" Guests (2022)

"Hates Kids" A Cup of Comfort for Mothers (2010)

"Burying Bea" A Cup of Comfort for the Grieving Heart

(2010)

"The Apology" A Cup of Comfort for Single Mothers

(2008)

ADVANCED REVIEWS

I just finished reading **Five Golden Rings**. It was fun to see Derrick and Sloan's names in print! Great job! ~ *Kendra Henson, Crime Never Takes a Holiday*

A big twist in **Five Golden Rings**. The story really held my attention because the sheriff has an autistic deputy who is really valuable at a crime scene. This anthology is well worth the time and money! ~ *Reader, Crime Never Takes a Holiday*

"**Five Golden Rings** allowed me to return to Stoneybrook and be reunited with the town's colorful characters. Reading novella's is a challenge for me since I love spending more time in a story. But **Kimila Kay** kept me engaged and left me longing to return to Stoneybrook soon." ~ *Sharon North*

Five Golden Rings is an intriguing holiday story, and I couldn't wait to know who killed Santa. With each book I've read, **Kimila Kay** has honed her writing skills and continues to craft engaging tales. I can't wait for her next release, whether it's set in Mexico or in the adorable town of Stoneybrook. ~ *Ruth DeHaven, Crime Never Takes a Holiday*

FIVE GOLDEN RINGS

A Novella

STONEYBROOK MYSTERIES-BOOK TWO

KIMILA KAY

www.KimilaKay.com - author@kimilakay.com
Windtree Press - http://windtreepress.com
info@windtreepress.com

Cover Art by *James McCracken*
Five Golden Rings, Stoneybrook Mysteries,2

Published in the United States of America – History: ISBN 978-1-962065-22-1
1st Release: October 31, 2023

DEDICATION

For all of you who choose to believe, as Deputy Derrick Stone believes, in the wonderment and magic of Christmas.

"Our hearts grow tender with childhood memories and love of kindred, and we are better throughout the year for having, in spirit, become a child again at Christmastime." ~ *Laura Ingalls Wilder*

FIVE GOLDEN RINGS

CHAPTER ONE

"Holy holidays!" Deputy Barnes lifted his cap and scratched his graying buzz cut. "It looks like Christmas threw up in here."

Wyatt Stone scowled at his deputy, then knelt by the body lying under the Christmas tree. A pool of blood stained the decorative snow scene of the tree skirt. When he moved the tree's branches, a sweet, pine smell from the branches filled the room. Now, Barnes had a better look at Wallace Dunn, the retired hardware store owner who also served as Stoneybrook's resident Santa Claus.

"Oh, man." Barnes leaned over to get a better look, the buttons on his tan shirt straining to contain his girth. "Old man Dunn?" He huffed an expletive, a sharp contrast to the rendition of "O Come, All Ye Faithful" which played on the radio.

Wyatt pulled a glove from his shirt pocket and lifted Dunn's left hand. It was still in a tight fist—except for an index finger now set at an odd angle. He turned the arm over and studied the other fingers. The fist wasn't closed tightly, as if Dunn had been holding something.

"What'cha got there, Sheriff?" Barnes asked over Wyatt's shoulder.

"Not sure." Wyatt held out an open palm to Barnes. "Do you have an evidence bag?"

"Yep." Barnes placed the small plastic sack and a zip tie into Wyatt's hand.

Wyatt secured the bag over Dunn's fist, took the second setup from Barnes, and repeated the process. He stood and stepped back from the body, surveying the crime scene one last time. He knew the techs would process everything thoroughly, but Derrick had taught him to pay attention to every detail right from the start. Good advice since his autistic cousin always caught something the techs missed— thanks to his photographic memory.

Wyatt headed for the front door; Barnes close on his heels.

"Who'd do such a thing, Sheriff?"

"I guess it's up to us to find out who." Wyatt stepped onto the porch. Holiday lights twinkled over his head. "And why."

"Right." Barnes snitched a sugar cookie from the coffee table, then followed Wyatt.

"What's first, Chief?" Simms asked.

Wyatt ran a hand over his stubble. "The most important thing is to keep Derrick out of the crime scene."

"Jumping jingle bells!" Barnes's rosy cheeks darkened. "He won't handle Santa being stabbed and left under a Christmas tree very well."

"Agreed." Wyatt headed down the steps. "Simms, you stand guard over the house and wait for CSU."

"Copy, Chief." Simms gave Wyatt a head nod.

Wyatt headed for his truck, Barnes following him. "Barnes, I need you to canvas the neighborhood while I go to the hospital and interview Mercy Edwards."

"I thought this was her house." Barnes jotted in his notepad. "She found Santa?"

"Yes. Said she heard loud noises." Wyatt continued to his vehicle. "Called 911, grabbed her handgun, and made her way to the living room."

Barnes added more notes. "Was she hurt?"

"No." Wyatt angled into the driver's seat. "By the time she entered the room, the killer was running, and Dunn was dead."

"So no description of the perp?" Barnes asked.

Wyatt shook his head. "She was in shock, so I sent her to the hospital." He fired up the engine. "I'll see what she remembers."

"Got it." Barnes tucked his notepad into his shirt pocket. "Meet you back at the station."

"Copy," Wyatt said. He closed his door and backed out of the driveway. Barnes headed toward Simms and Wyatt knew they'd rehash what little details they'd gleaned so far.

Wyatt and Derrick had been each other's family for some years now, so Christmas was spent either working or being invited to friends' homes for dinner. But Wyatt always made sure there were presents under a tall, decorated Noble fir. His wrapped gift for Derrick would sit next to the gift his cousin had selected for him. Derrick had an uncanny ability to pick perfect gifts, from personal items like last year's wallet to the *Oregon Moonshine* book for the lodge the year before. But the highlight of Christmas morning was the look of wonder on Derrick's face when unwrapped gifts from the list he'd given Wyatt on the first of September sat under the tree.

Dread washed over Wyatt as he thought about what needed to happen next. Telling Deputy Derrick Stone that Santa had been murdered could possibly cause his cousin to lose control of his tightly-maintained composure.

CHAPTER TWO

"Why couldn't Dunn let it go?" He back-kicked the front door closed. "Damn it!" He tossed the bloody knife on top of the dirty dishes in the sink and turned on the hot water. Pink rivulets ran down the drain as he rubbed his hands together. The metallic smell of blood mingled with the sour smell of days-old food. He rinsed the dishes and fed them into the dishwasher, adding the murder weapon to the top rack, then pushed start.

"Shit!" He reached for the fifth of whiskey and took a long swig, coughing when the liquor burned the back of his throat. Dropping into a chair, he took another drink, then placed the bottle on the small dining table. It was possible the old fool knew nothing and had just happened upon the ring at the pawn shop. What had Dunn told the customer in his hardware store? "An early Christmas present for a special someone."

"What the hell am I going to do now?" Stupid question, because he knew he had to leave Stoneybrook. He'd been running his whole life, his past always nipping at his heels. But first, he had to figure out what Wallace Dunn knew. *Did he have any proof? Had he told anyone? Would the Sheriff be on his trail now?*

He reached for the whiskey bottle and tipped it to his lips, then shouted, "I seen to it that he cain't say anything now!" The liquor warmed his cheeks and lit a fire in the pit of his stomach. He'd always been good at masking his darker side, blending into small communities, and living a boring normal life.

However, when his long-buried secrets could be exposed, he had no choice except to silence the person who would reveal his alter ego.

CHAPTER THREE

"Perfect!" Harley said, admiring the lacy cream-colored angel perched atop the ten-foot Noble Fir. She circled the living room of her old farmhouse and lit cinnamon-scented candles. It was her first Christmas on the Redneck Ranch. First holiday away from New York. First without her mom, Esther and brother, Harris.

"There will be no sadness." She lifted a crystal mug of eggnog in a toast to her decorating skills.

The large antique grandfather clock chimed indicating the time was now half-past six. Everything was ready for her holiday party. She just needed to change, so she headed for the staircase and climbed up to her bedroom.

This soiree would be so different from the endless celebrations she'd attended in New York, and she was a tad nervous.

"No," she told her reflection as she touched up her makeup. "I think I nailed it." She lifted her long, dark curls off her neck with a sparkly red ribbon. "Just the right touch of elegance to compliment the laid-back charm of Stoneybrook."

Harley smacked her lips together then blotted the red lipstick with a tissue. With one last glance in the full-length mirror, she smiled and fingered the pretty horses at the center of her necklace. The jewelry set, which included a matching bracelet and lightning bolt earrings, was an early Christmas present from Wyatt. A sweet gesture, which would have been even sweeter if it had been accompanied by a love note. Instead, he'd penned a simple *Merry Early Christmas, Ms. Harper* on the notecard. Their budding six-month romance was still as exciting as when Wyatt had first kissed her. Harley knew she was in love with him, so she longed to hear those words from his lips.

Or was she rushing herself and the handsome sheriff? Did she need those three magic words to erase the pain Archer Shaw had caused when he'd stranded her at the altar? Maybe she wanted Wyatt to say what she felt before she blurted it out in a moment of passion.

Harley stopped her musings and refocused on her attire, which she crafted to compliment the turquoise and dark red stones set in the necklace. Now that she lived in Oregon, she wanted to dress accordingly. She'd found the perfect navy blue, cropped Pendleton sweater, which she wore with a white scoop-neck T-shirt. Jeans had never been part of her holiday attire; however, she liked the way the dark-wash Wranglers hugged her ass. Besides the jewelry, the best part of her ensemble was the pair of silver-studded red Corral boots she'd bought herself for Christmas.

She heard the front door open, followed by, "Har Har?"

"Coming!" Harley headed for the stairs, bounding down to meet her childhood friend, Busy.

Trampas, the mutt Harley had inherited with the ranch, danced around Busy. She was slipping off brown leather gloves in the foyer, surrounded by her luggage. "Seriously, Harley." Busy began unbuttoning her caramel-colored coat. "What's the point of it being so damn cold without snow?"

"I'm so glad you came!" Harley hugged her bestie. "How was your trip?" Trampas scratched and fluffed the dog bed that was tucked in a corner of the living room.

Shucking her coat and hanging it on the coat rack, Busy declared, "That story is going to require a glass of champagne." She fluffed her shoulder-length blonde curls and headed for the kitchen.

"Umm," Harley trailed after Busy. "I have eggnog, hot mulled wine, and beer."

Busy stopped abruptly and spun around. "Beer?"

Harley nodded and continued to the kitchen. "Some deliciously cold microbrews."

"God help us!" Busy sat in a chair at the drop-leaf table and tapped her phone. "I'll just have a few bottles delivered from the Rocky River Bar."

"Umm." Harley tried to suppress a smile as she crossed to the fridge.

"Let me guess." Busy set her phone down. "No deliveries this late in the quaint little town of Stoneybrook?" Her New York accent elongated her vowels.

"Claire's having a hard time getting deliveries. She said her alcohol stock is sorely lacking." Harley pulled two bottles of Kris Kringle ale from the fridge and popped the caps. "I promise you're going to love this," she said, placing a bottle adorned with a colorful Santa in front of Busy. She wrinkled her nose as Harley took a healthy swig and sat down.

Sniffing the ale as if it were a glass of red wine, Busy finally took a small sip. "Well, it's not terrible."

The friends clinked the bottles together and drank some beer.

"I got a Christmas card from Sadie too." Busy pointed to the collection of cards taped to the hutch that sat behind Harley in the dining room. "She said Santa is bringing her a horse for Christmas."

"That's what she wrote in my card too." Harley took another sip. "I miss having her around, but I'm glad she and her family are doing well in Wyoming."

"Is Sadie still in counseling?" Busy tipped the bottle to her lips.

"According to Wyatt who talks regularly to Sadie's Aunt Melanie, the whole family is getting counseling." Harley smiled.

"Good. Sometimes the best way to start over is to get your head straight." Busy sipped more beer. "So, who all is coming to this shindig?"

"Everyone you met when you were here in May," Harley said. "Not a large crowd. And I didn't invite Ace."

Busy's face scrunched into a frown, and she changed the subject. "A far cry from our bashes back in "The City That Never Sleeps.""

Harley reached across the table and touched her bestie's arm. "We did have some great parties."

"Nothing's the same anymore without you, Harley." Busy flipped a clump of curls from her shoulder. "That bastard, Archer, has come to a few events, but it was so effing awkward that our circle of friends sort of imploded." Busy took a long pull from her beer. "Enough of that bullshit." She aimed her finger at Harley and made a couple of circles. "Is the handsome sheriff behind this look?"

Heat warmed Harley's cheeks and she touched her necklace. "Maybe."

"Well, it suits you." Busy took another sip. "Never thought I'd see you out of your favorite silver sequined mini, but I like this look."

"Thanks. You look great too."

Busy stood and did a slow pirouette, showing off her champagne-colored pantsuit, the beaded jacket shimmering like diamonds. "Of course I do," Busy laughed and resumed her seat. "So did the necklace come with an 'I love you?'"

"Elizabeth Benton!" Harley narrowed her eyes. "It's only been—"

"Don't full name me, Harley Harper." Busy held up a finger. "I saw the way he looked at you when I was here and—"

A knock sounded on the front door and Harley jumped to her feet. "Company's here!"

She hurried to the foyer and opened the door to find her vets, Ella Night and Hannah Sloan, escorted by Hannah's husband, Luke.

"Come in," Harley invited, and they stepped into the foyer. Luke held a bottle of red wine and Hannah cradled a red poinsettia plant.

"Miss Bonnie just dropped off Derrick." Ella held a plate of Christmas cookies. She looked behind her, then back at Harley. "He's standing on the porch."

Harley stepped outside. Derrick huddled in his coat, hands shoved into the pockets. Harley knew Wyatt's cousin sometimes had trouble with crowds, which was why she'd kept the guest list small and invited only people he knew.

"Derrick." Harley stood still, since he could be wary of sudden movement.

"Miss Bonnie said to say she's sorry she couldn't stay." Derrick looked at his watch. "The boardinghouse Christmas party is also tonight."

"Yes, she told me." Harley moved closer. "Would you like to come in?"

"Not seven yet." He stuck his hand back into his pocket.

"Yes, except I already have guests inside, so you should come in out of the cold."

Derrick bobbed his head and checked his watch again. "At seven."

Harley peeked over her shoulder at the grandfather clock, which showed one minute to seven. "Okay," she said and backed into the foyer.

Before she could tell everyone to make themselves comfortable, the old clock began its seven chimes, accompanied by a sharp knock.

Harley opened the door again. Without a word, Derrick stepped inside, followed by Cedar Atwood.

"I'm so glad you could both come." Harley smiled, then added, "Can I take everyone's coats?"

Luke, Hannah, and Ella had already removed theirs. Derrick shook his head as Cedar, who preferred to be called by her nickname Echo, handed Harley her red wool coat. She was glad Echo had come to her party. Wyatt had told her the holidays were hard for the young woman. Her sister, Willow, was still missing after being abducted over four years ago.

Busy joined Harley at the coat closet. "I'm guessing there's a good reason you didn't invite Ace."

Harley met her friend's questioning stare and parted her lips to offer the excuse she'd prepared. Before she could speak, Busy held up a finger.

"Never mind, he must be seeing someone. But knowing you, you planned to give me a different explanation."

"Busy—"

Busy waved her off. "Let's get comfy."

Her beige-colored heels thudded against the polished oak floor as she crossed to the living room. Hannah had set the poinsettia on the coffee table. Ella offered Busy a cookie before placing the plate next to the plant.

"I'll take that." Busy smiled, and Luke handed her the bottle of cabernet. "I don't suppose you have a bottle of champagne tucked into your back pocket?" She laughed at her joke.

"No ma'am," Luke responded.

"Ma'am!" Busy waved off the moniker. "You know me well enough to call me Busy."

Ella looked at her phone. "Britt's on his way and apologizes for being late."

"I'm glad he's able to come," Harley said as she joined them. "I know he's been working hard to repair the water damage done to Pebbles and Pretties from the broken pipes."

Derrick had moved into the front room too. He smoothed his short sandy- hair, and she knew he was looking for Wyatt. It was now five past the hour, and she understood Wyatt's job sometimes made it a challenge to be on time. A wisp of concern flickered through her mind since his deputies hadn't arrived either. And what could be keeping Claire and Mercy? She'd become used to the promptness of Stoneybrook residents. This was a busy time of year, though, so perhaps everyone was just running late.

Luke's phone chirped with an incoming text. He looked at his phone and the wisp of concern morphed into a cloud of worry when Harley saw the look on Luke's face.

CHAPTER FOUR

The whiskey bottle fell to the cracked linoleum floor, startling him awake. His foggy brain struggled to process where he was, then the night's events careened through his mind like a wild pinball.

Wallace Dunn's crumpled body flashed before his eyes, and his sickening yowl filled the small dining room as if the dead man were already haunting him.

"Why did he have to buy that ring?" He stumbled to the fridge and yanked it open, covering his nose when the stench of soured milk assailed him. He was hungry, but the only items on the shelves were three cans of beer, a half loaf of moldy bread, and an almost-empty jar of dill pickles.

He cracked open a beer and guzzled half the contents, then scrubbed his hand over his face, wincing at the thought of having to go out in public. Since he'd have to stay in Stoneybrook for a couple of weeks he'd have to venture out at some point before he could disappear—again.

He would give anything to be able to stay and enjoy the holidays with the few friends he'd made here. But no, he had to pawn one of the rings. While the other four were worth more, they all had large jewels or unique characteristics. He'd forgotten that the plainest of the five rings had a small etching on the inside of the band: *Always & Forever*. He stumbled into the shabby living room of his rented house and stood in front of the blackened red-brick fireplace. He nudged the loose brick just under the mantel and slid it free, easing the black cloth bag from the tiny space.

Looking inside, he wondered if the dead women's families had all reported the missing jewelry. Even after all this time, he could match a face to each ring. The stunning one-and-a-half carat marquis belonged to the buxom blonde with ice blue eyes that he'd stalked for three weeks before finally enjoying her loveliness. The princess cut rimmed with sapphires had been worn by a thin waif with long, jet black hair. He'd wanted to enjoy the chase, but when she confronted him about following her, he'd forced her into his truck, rushed his pleasure, and ended her life on a deserted back road. The snotty, red-headed bitch who'd worn the vintage cushion-cut diamond perched in a white gold halo setting had called him a filthy animal. He'd responded with a viciousness that left her whimpering, but she would not beg for her life.

His favorite had been the wearer of the yellow, oval diamond set in a white gold band glimmering with smaller cuts. He closed his eyes, her face swimming behind his lids.

He imagined he could still smell her perfume, something citrusy that made him think of summer. He settled on the memory of her long, brown hair. She was always sweeping her bangs from her hazel eyes. She was exquisite and elegant, always quick with a smile and a hug when she greeted someone. And she wasn't pretentious.

He opened his eyes and sighed, again wishing his urge to have her hadn't grown into such a frenzy, so he could have studied her for a longer time. She'd been his last, so extraordinary he'd convinced himself he could never exceed her perfection. So, for eighteen long months, he hadn't fed his dark side, hiding in plain sight among the residents of Stoneybrook.

And now what might be his undoing was the simple gold band set with three round stones. The ring belonged to a plain-looking young girl with flaxen hair. She wasn't his usual taste, except something about her confidence had intrigued him. He'd stalked her before discovering his hazel-eyed goddess. But once again his desire overwhelmed him, and she became his *always and forever* on a dark summer night.

He knew he had to leave Stoneybrook, so maybe he should treat himself to a parting gift. The young waitress who worked at the Babbling Brook Café? Or the Native American bartender at the Rocky River Bar? And then there was the beautiful owner of the Redneck Ranch.

CHAPTER FIVE

Wyatt Stone waited in the hallway while a nurse tended to Mercy Edwards. The owner of the Babbling Brook Café looked pale, which made her gray hair seem a shade darker. The nurse exited the room, and Mercy smiled at Wyatt as he stepped toward the bed.

"Sheriff," Mercy said, her voice quivering. "Is it true?" Tears pooled in her eyes, and she used the bedsheet to dab them away.

Wyatt removed his cowboy hat and nodded. "I'm afraid so, Mercy."

A sob escaped her lips. She leaned back and closed her eyes. Wyatt waited a minute, then took her hand in his.

Sorrow clouded Mercy's eyes when she opened them again. It made Wyatt wish he had a softer touch when it came to dealing with survivors of murdered loved ones. Until this moment, he hadn't known the depth of the friendship between Mercy and Wallace. For a fleeting second, he winced at the thought of Harley being *his* survivor.

Setting his feelings aside, he fidgeted with his hat and began his query. "Can you answer a few questions for me?"

Mercy sat up taller. "Yes."

"You were expecting Wallace for dinner?" Wyatt knew to be short and specific.

She nodded and her face grew mottled, but she managed to contain another wave of tears.

"Was he contributing anything to the meal?"

Mercy looked confused. "No. I'd fixed a honey-glazed ham, scalloped potatoes, green salad, and rolls." She smoothed the hospital blanket. "Oh, and mincemeat pie for dessert."

"Were you and Wallace exchanging gifts?"

Another look of bewilderment crossed Mercy's face. She shook her head. "No. Why?"

Wyatt hesitated. "Just a routine question."

The tilt of Mercy's head told him she thought he was lying but he didn't want to insinuate Wallace had bought her a gift. Especially since he had no idea what had been clutched so tightly in the old guy's hand.

A doctor knuckle-rapped the door and stepped into the room. "How are you feeling?" she asked, touching the monitor screen of a computer.

"I'm fine," Mercy stated in a calm tone. "I'd like to go home now."

The doctor moved to the bed and offered a sympathetic smile. "I understand you've had a rough evening." She cast a look at Wyatt, then returned her attention to Mercy. "I'm new to the area and I've heard nice things about Mr. Dunn."

Mercy's face crumpled and the doctor patted her hand. "I'll send a nurse in with your discharge paperwork." The doctor turned to Wyatt and extended her hand. "Maggie Anderson."

He shook her hand. "Wyatt Stone."

"Are you Miss Edwards' ride home, Sheriff?"

"No, no," Mercy said waving a hand. "Sheriff Stone has more important business to attend to. My friend Claire Norman is picking me up."

Wyatt looked at his watch. 7:30. He knew Deputy Barnes would've texted Luke by now, although he couldn't be sure Luke had explained his absence to Harley. If Claire was Mercy's ride, then maybe she'd alerted Harley to the situation.

A nurse entered the room as Doctor Anderson made her exit. The doctor nearly ran into Claire Norman, who was hurrying to Mercy's bedside.

"Oh, Hun." Claire wrapped her arms around Mercy who let loose a flood of tears. "It's going to be okay."

Glad to leave the bitter, antiseptic smell of the hospital behind, Wyatt made his exit. The two old friends clung to each other, and he knew they'd eventually be fine, but *okay* would be harder to achieve. That was something he'd learned personally after his parents died.

His phone buzzed with an incoming text. He expected it to be from Harley.

Barnes: *Crime scene techs found an empty ring box tucked into one of the tree limbs.*

Wyatt: *Prints?*

Barnes: *Unlikely.*

Wyatt: *Anything else?*

Barnes: *Not yet.*

Wyatt: *Keep me posted. Headed to Harley's.*

Barnes: *Copy*

Wyatt slipped his phone back into his shirt pocket and headed for his truck. He knew he needed to be at Harley's, but dreaded dealing with the meltdown Derrick would have once he was told about Santa's death.

CHAPTER SIX

Harley had tasked Derrick with bringing more firewood to the front porch. Normally, she'd have him bring a couple of loads into the living room and stack the pieces into the cubby built into the brick fireplace. But she instinctively knew that when Luke shared what was in the text he'd received, Derrick needed to be out of earshot.

Luke added another log to the fire, the smoky aroma blending with the cinnamon-scented candles.

Tell us, Luke." The dread on Hannah's face was reflected in her husband's eyes.

"It's Wallace Dunn," Luke said. "Someone killed him."

Harley's phone chimed and she pulled it from her back pocket.

Wyatt: *On my way.*

"What the eff!" Busy looked around the room, then at Harley. "Who's Wallace Dunn? And why would someone kill him at Christmastime for gawd sake?"

"He owns the hardware store and serves as Stoneybrook's Santa during the holidays," Hannah said as she stepped into Luke's arms.

"Who's going to tell Derrick?" Echo asked.

"Wyatt's on his way." Harley slipped her phone back into her pocket. "We just need to keep Derrick busy until Wyatt gets here."

"Because?" Eyebrows raised, Busy took a sip of cabernet. "Surely he doesn't still believe in Santa."

"Yes, he does," Echo nodded, "believe in Santa."

"It's complicated," Harley said as she peeked through the decorative glass sidelight next to the large front door. She could see Derrick standing next to the woodshed.

Busy looked over Harley's shoulder. "So is he going to cry or something?"

"Derrick loves all the holidays, but especially Christmas, so this news will be hard for him to process." Stepping away from the door, Harley retrieved her phone and replied to Wyatt's text.

Harley: *ETA?*

The Redneck Ranch sat about five miles outside of Stoneybrook, so it shouldn't take him long to arrive. And after dating for six months, Harley had learned Sheriff Wyatt Stone would dive right into investigative mode.

CHAPTER SEVEN

Wyatt had parked his vehicle on the road, then walked slowly up the dark driveway, trying to delay the inevitable delivery of bad news. He stood in the crisp, cold air and watched Derrick tidy the stack of wood against the house's front wall.

He admired his cousin's attention to small things. Derrick would make sure each log was properly tucked into the intricate puzzle, assuring the stack would not fall over when the top piece of wood was plucked free.

Wyatt strode forward and climbed the weathered porch steps, the creaking old boards announcing his arrival. Derrick adjusted the last section of wood, then turned and faced Wyatt.

His cousin consulted his watch. "You are forty minutes late."

"Sorry." Wyatt pointed toward two wicker chairs. "Can we sit for a minute before we go inside?"

Derrick hesitated, then sat on the edge of a chair with his hands on his knees. A familiar posture Wyatt knew meant his deputy was anticipating the need to flee. There was no easy way to tell someone about the death of a loved one, or in this case, the death of a kind man who nurtured the whimsical magic of Christmas.

"You should talk," Derrick said without looking at Wyatt.

Might as well get this over with, Wyatt thought. "There's been a murder."

Derrick gave Wyatt an alert stare. "Who?"

Wyatt steeled himself and continued, "Wallace Dunn."

"No. No. NO!" Derrick jumped to his feet and began to pace. "No! Not Santa!" He pummeled his head with both fists. "No! No! No!"

Generally, these outbursts only lasted for a minute or two. But it was possible his cousin might completely lose control and be unable to help with the investigation.

Derrick stopped abruptly, red-faced, with tears pooling in his eyes. Knowing not to move suddenly, Wyatt slowly came to his feet. He also knew Derrick didn't like to be touched, so offering a consoling hug was out of the question. Like it or not, waiting for Derrick to decide what happened next was the best course of action.

The front door cracked open behind him. Harley stood in the doorway and Wyatt glanced at her. He held up a finger and turned his attention back to Derrick.

"Harley," Derrick marched toward the porch steps. "We're sorry to miss your party, but Wyatt and I have a murder to solve." His boots thumped against the stairs as he made his way to the walkway.

Harley stepped from the house and Wyatt turned to her. "Go," she said, "and please keep me posted."

Wyatt closed the distance between them in quick strides. He removed his hat and kissed her, a hint of wine on her breath. He savored the comfort of her lips and wished he could stay.

But he had a job to do, so he met her concerned stare and said, "Will do, Ms. Harper." He touched the horses on her necklace, then trudged after Derrick.

CHAPTER EIGHT

As she went about her chores, Harley felt as though even her menagerie was lacking the holiday spirit. Her efforts to bring festivity to the animal barn with lights and a small tree didn't seem to help. Or maybe this was how animals responded to the dark days of winter, huddled in their stalls enjoying the warmth of infrared heaters and dreaming of sunnier days.

She greeted each creature with a cheery, "Merry Christmas," as she fed them their breakfast. Pigmy goat siblings, Butch and Sundance flicked their tails, but were missing the flounce in their step. Hoss, her old hog, didn't bother to react to her greeting. Her minis, Rhett and Scarlett sidled up to their gate for a drive by pat, the focused on their alfalfa. Maverick brayed his Christmas greeting and extended his neck for his flake of hay.

"Merry Christmas, Maverick." Harley scratched his ears, then moved to Trigger's stall. The sorrel quarter horse stepped to the Dutch door gate and pointed his nose at Harley. "How does a little alfalfa sound for Christmas cheer, Trigger?" Harley placed the flake in his bin.

Last to receive a holiday wish was Elvis, her large, black horse. Elvis had already stuck his head over the gate and waited for her to hold her palm up to complete their usual greeting. "Hey, big guy. Hungry?" Elvis tossed his head and nickered when she added his hay to the feeding bin.

Harley turned and gave the barn a parting glance. "Merry Christmas, Menagerie."

As she walked back to the house, she thought about the days following the murder. Stoneybrook didn't seem infused with the normal festive spirit Christmastime usually brought. Most residents stayed home, leaving the festively decorated Pebbles and Pretties mercantile with gift-stocked shelves and the trendy Streams and Meadows restaurant without dinner reservations. And she knew the same question she asked herself was on everyone else's lips: *Who among them was a killer?*

Some neighborhoods remained dressed in holiday finery with twinkling lights strung on eaves and manger scenes adorning their lawns. A large Douglas fir stood tall in front of city hall, with a glowing star shining through the night, but the tree's Christmas lights seemed diminished in the wake of the tragedy.

Harley knew firsthand how resilient the residents of Stoneybrook could be. The town had helped save her ranch from a raging fire. Wyatt and his deputies had finally solved the mysterious murders of three young women spanning a seven-year period, and Harley was no longer afraid of the ancient barn where two of the bodies were found. Still, though, the town was missing one of its own. She knew Wyatt hadn't given up hope of finding Willow Atwood.

She tried to drum up the holiday spirit, for her own sake and Busy's, but it was hard not to feel cheated of all she'd imagined for her first Christmas with Wyatt. She'd envisioned a Norman Rockwell holiday with her cowboy, complete with caroling, so she could enjoy Wyatt's beautiful baritone singing voice. A white Christmas, which was rare in Stoneybrook. Cuddling on the couch in front of a warm fire.

But her dashing sheriff was needed elsewhere.

She inhaled the comforting scent of the molasses cookies Busy had place in the oven. Harley sighed and wrapped the last gift, thinking about poor Wallace Dunn. He'd been respected and well-liked in Stoneybrook, so it was inconceivable that anyone who lived in the quaint burg could be responsible.

But a murderer did indeed walk among them, and the citizens of Stoneybrook were terrified he'd strike again.

CHAPTER NINE

Finally, he had a plan. In three days, on Christmas Eve, he'd leave a parting gift for Sheriff Stone and be on his way to a new adventure.

He'd been following the beguiling Harley Harper throughout Stoneybrook as she shopped for groceries at DairyMart, bought Christmas presents, and chatted with Mercy Edwards while he ate his usual ham and egg scramble.

He was thankful he hadn't had to kill the owner of the popular Babbling Brook Café, but he also worried she might've seen him. He doubted she had and killing an old woman wasn't of any interest to him. But he wouldn't hesitate if she started wagging her tongue. Since he wasn't aware that she'd said anything about a ring, he was beginning to believe Wallace Dunn had kept the purchase of the ring a secret.

Today, Harley and her blonde friend had taken time to visit with the owner of Pebbles and Pretties, Mia Davis. Harley had eventually picked out a pair of leather gloves, which he assumed were intended for the Sheriff. Too bad she'd not see him open the gift Christmas morning.

And speaking of gifts, what would he take from the lovely Harley as a memento? He'd seen her wear a ring once—a pear-shaped ruby set in a gold band, accentuated by small diamonds. While he knew the best present Harley had to offer was herself, he doubted she would do so freely. But then that was the whole point to this dance. The hunt. The capture. The reward.

His loins burned as he imagined exploring the wonder of Harley Harper. Claiming her lips as she tried to protest his kisses. Inhaling the musky scent between her breasts. Running his hands over every inch of her soft skin before taking her treasure. Then leaving her naked, plundered body beneath the majestic Douglas fir as a parting present for Sheriff Stone and the good people of Stoneybrook.

CHAPTER TEN

"It's a fair assumption Dunn was holding a ring in his hand when he was stabbed," Barnes said as he jotted *ring* in bold letters onto the chalkboard, punctuated by a question mark.

"Right, considering we have an empty jewelry box." Simms set the coffee maker to brew, the dark roast blend wafting through the office.

Barnes added *box* to the board. "Except we haven't been able to find any confirmation that Dunn bought a ring. No receipt in his house. No record of purchase at any of the major jewelers from Portland to Salem, or the towns in between."

Tapping a page in his little black book, Simms added, "And Dunn didn't have an Amazon account, either."

"What about pawnshops?" Wyatt asked, knowing the answer but asking to be thorough.

"If a shop has no record of a sale." Derrick paced the bullpen area of the station. "Then the ring was stolen."

Coming to a halt at the front of the station, he stared out the large picture window. "I believe this is the case because the gift box is shabby, probably second-hand."

Derrick had spent every day since the murder studying the evidence, crime scene photos, and coroner's report. While the team used the chalkboard to flesh out the details, Derrick filled pages in a spiral-bound notebook with different scenarios of the crime.

Barnes printed *shabby* next to *box* and circled the word.

"We need to scour past murders to see if there is a connection to a missing ring." Wyatt stood. "Derrick, can I have a word?"

Barnes and Simms, each with a donut in hand, returned to their respective desks and began punching the keys on their computers. Derrick made his way across the bullpen, followed Wyatt into his office, and closed the door.

Wyatt sat behind his desk, not bothering to suggest Derrick sit. He knew his cousin was too wound up to do so.

"Do you have a profile yet?" Wyatt asked.

Derrick briefly met Wyatt's stare, then glanced past him through the window behind his chair and began to list possible attributes of Dunn's killer.

"White male. Twenty-five to Thirty. Single. Menial Job. Transient, just passing through Stoneybrook." He paused, tilted his head slightly, then looked at Wyatt. "I don't think the murder was planned. But a spontaneous act due to circumstances."

"Circumstances?" Wyatt repeated.

"I believe the killer felt he had no choice." Derrick briefly looked at Wyatt, then back out the window. "I think the killer brought a weapon, probably to threaten Dunn, but then murdered him instead."

"Maybe Dunn knew his killer," Wyatt speculated.

"Or Dunn took something the killer wanted back."

"Like a stolen ring?"

Derrick nodded. "Also, we got a hit on our BOLO for Willow.

Wyatt straightened in his chair. "Tell me."

"A Christmas tree lot in Eureka, California called the local police saying they thought a young woman matching Willow's description bought a tree earlier this week." Derrick held Wyatt's stare.

"And?" Wyatt prodded, reminding himself to be patient.

"The woman was alone and bought a dried out tree for ten dollars." Derrick stood. "She paid cash and dragged the tree behind her when she left."

"Are the police following up at grocery stores, gas stat—"

"Yes." Derrick cut him off, then exited Wyatt's office. Barnes angled his way inside, his face scrunched as if he'd sucked on a lemon.

"What?" Wyatt barked.

"Blake's here," Barnes said and retreated.

Wyatt's cheeks burned hot at the mention of his brother's name. They hadn't spoken in over a year, and he'd been just fine with the silence. Now that he'd met Harley, Wyatt could see Ava Parker had not been worth the trouble. After Wyatt and Ava had dated for six months, she'd chosen Blake over him. As far as he was concerned, the two of them could go straight to hell.

"Barnes said you were free." Blake Stone stood in the doorway, hands in his pockets, a flicker of defiance in his aqua eyes.

Wyatt stood. "I'm on my way out." He grabbed his gun from a drawer and holstered it. "You've got until I reach my truck to state your business."

Blake stepped in front of Wyatt, blocking his exit. The two brothers stood toe-to-toe, similar blue eyes locked in a stare down.

"What do you want?" Wyatt growled, his hands balled into fists.

"I heard about Dunn's murder and thought I could help." Blake's tone had the same sharp edge as Wyatt's.

"My deputies and I don't need a bounty hunter's help." Wyatt bumped Blake's shoulder as he pushed past him.

Continuing, Blake followed him. "I think Dunn's killer is responsible for other murders spanning several states."

Wyatt stopped at the station doors, then turned and glared at Blake. "You have any proof?"

Blake nodded. Barnes drew a line down the center of the chalkboard and printed *Serial* at the top of the new column. Simms turned his chair to face the board. Derrick stood at the opposite end of the chalkboard, notepad in hand, pen at the ready.

Wyatt knew his deputies were making the right call. Any information Blake might have would need to be vetted and matched to what they already knew—or had eliminated.

"Give him the chalk," Wyatt said to Barnes, then turned a chair around, straddled it, and sat down.

Blake stepped to the board, scribbled the number one, then California, and the name Sara Howard.

Wyatt forced his anger aside and gestured for his little brother to begin. Whatever their differences, Blake had been a good deputy. While not as good an investigator as Derrick, he had the ability to see a case from yet another perspective. If they had a serial killer in their town, then it was all hands on deck to protect the citizens of Stoneybrook.

CHAPTER ELEVEN

With three days until Christmas, a pall hung over the town after the murder of poor Wallace Dunn, and subsequent death of Santa. But some residents still said, "Merry Christmas," as they moved about browsing for gifts, having lunch, or enjoying a cup of holiday cheer.

After a morning filled with cleaning stalls and feeding animals, Harley and Busy sat in a booth at the Babbling Brook Café. Busy had insisted on staying until the end of December instead of returning to New York after the failed holiday party, claiming Harley would need the distraction of company while Wyatt was solving a murder.

"I know it's not on my diet, but the Hammy sandwich sounds to die for!" Busy said from behind her menu.

"It's a good choice." Mercy stood at their table, order pad and pen in hand.

"How are you, Mercy?" Harley asked.

A whisp of sadness shone in her eyes. "Fine, dear." Mercy smoothed her apron. "Wallace was such a kind man. It's hard to imagine why anyone would want him dead." A tear trickled down her cheek and she fingered it away. "Now, what can I get you two?"

"I'll have the winter salad with balsamic vinaigrette," Harley said.

"You want to add grilled chicken?" Mercy asked.

"Yes, that would be great."

"And I'll have the Hammy sandwich with a side salad and ranch." Busy handed her menu to Mercy.

"Food will be right out." Mercy took Harley's menu too. "Are you good with water, or can I get you something more festive?"

"Do you happen to have champagne?" Busy asked.

Mercy nodded. "A special prosecco, pomegranate mimosa to celebrate Christmas." Her voice trailed off as if no one should be celebrating the holidays.

"Perfect!" Busy clapped her hands together.

"Two specials coming up," Mercy said as she headed for the order counter.

"Finally," Busy said with a beaming smile. "Champagne!"

"But doesn't it feel weird to—" Harley began.

"Don't *but* me!" Busy narrowed her eyes. "We've done nothing *but* speculate about who murdered Santa, which has only served to depress the hell out of everyone. It's time to enjoy a little holiday cheer."

"You're right." Harley smiled as a waitress placed the pretty bubbly drinks in front of them. She picked up her glass. "Here's to as merry a Christmas as possible!"

"Speaking of *marry*." Busy drilled Harley with her eyes. "I know Archer hurt you terribly and you want to be happy again, but don't go confessing your love for Wyatt before his macho ass says it first."

"I'm not—" Harley began.

"Of course, you're in love with him!" Busy interjected. "You were in love with him from that first kiss last summer. But you have to wait him out."

Busy held up her flute. After a moment, Harley clinked her glass. They sipped in silence for a few minutes. Harley knew Busy was right, and it would be better for Wyatt to declare his love for her first. Besides, as much as she adored him, her life in Stoneybrook was still new. If spending her future with a handsome cowboy was in the cards, she'd just have to wait for the right hand to be dealt.

Their food arrived and Busy gushed, "Oh my, this smells delicious!"

Harley nodded and added the dressing to her salad. She wasn't very hungry. But she knew Busy would insist on another mimosa, so filling her stomach was necessary.

"This Hammy is so good," Busy said around a bite. "Maybe we should go to dinner tonight at Streams and Meadows? Keep our holiday groove going."

"That would be fun." Harley forked in a bite of chicken.

"Can Wyatt Earp join us?" Busy giggled at her joke.

"Funny." Harley said with an eye roll.

"Oh, come on!" Busy swallowed a cherry tomato. "You know you're handsome sheriff still looks like a younger version of Kurt Russell's character in *Tombstone*."

"I'm guessing he probably can't join us since he's hunting a killer in *Tombstone*."

"Right." Busy finished her mimosa and waggled her glass at the waitress. "Just you and me then? Or do you want to invite Claire and Mercy? Or the Sloan's, Ella, and Britt?"

"It could be fun to make it a little party since mine was cancelled." Harley choked on her mimosa.

"What?" Busy asked, her tone an octave higher than normal.

"Nothing." Harley shifted her gaze from the entrance and focused on her salad.

"Harley?" Blake asked.

She met his eyes, so like Wyatt's. Though she'd never met Blake in person, she recognized him from pictures she'd found tucked in a drawer in Wyatt's study. If she didn't know Wyatt was older by almost two years, she'd think the brothers were twins.

"Yes." Harley forced a smile and stood. "It's nice to finally meet you, Blake."

Busy also came to her feet. "Elizabeth Benton," she said and offered her hand.

"Nice to meet you." Blake shook her hand, then said to Harley, "Sorry to interrupt your lunch, I just want—"

"Blake." Mercy's tone suggested annoyance. "Where's Ava?"

"Mercy." Blake gave a slight smile. "Good to see you again."

Mercy narrowed her eyes at him. "I believe you've achieved your goal, now you need to be on your way."

Blake stiffened, and anger flashed in his eyes. "Enjoy your lunch, ladies." He gave Harley and Busy a slight bow, then made his exit.

"Good riddance," Mercy said as she marched off.

"Holy handsomeness!" Busy gave a low whistle. "What was that all about?"

"Long story." Harley finished her drink just as the waitress delivered two more.

"Like we have anywhere to be." Busy picked up her mimosa and leaned back in her chair.

"I only know what I've heard in gossip—because Wyatt doesn't talk about it. Evidently Blake ran off with a woman Wyatt was dating over a year ago."

"Do tell." Busy cozied up to the table.

Harley shrugged. "That's all I know." It wasn't the whole truth, since Wyatt's response when she'd asked about Ava had been, 'she's not you.' Harley could tell Ava's betrayal had hurt him deeply.

"How did Blake know who you are?" Busy sipped mimosa.

"I don't know. Wyatt does have a picture of me on his desk." Harley tilted her head. "Maybe Blake stopped at the station before coming here."

"Or gossip about you and Blake reached his brother wherever he's been hiding." Busy nodded toward the back of the restaurant. "What about the guy sitting at the counter?"

Harley turned to see, but the man had already disappeared through the door before she could get a good look. She shot a questioning glance at Busy.

"He's been watching you, or maybe us, since we sat down." Busy frowned. "I should've said something sooner."

"It's probably nothing," Harley said. "Maybe he was intrigued by your New York accent."

"Accent?" Busy laughed. "What'choo taakin about?"

Harley laughed too. Despite her effort to squelch her fear, tentacles of worry slithered down her spine and spiked her heart rate. She'd lived in Stoneybrook for seven months now and thought she knew most of the town folk, but the sight of the departing man had caused an uneasiness. Then again, the idea of a killer living in Stoneybrook probably just had her on edge. *Probably*, she silently repeated.

CHAPTER TWELVE

"Damn it!" He slammed the front door shut, the loud bang echoing through the ramshackle house. "I didn't want her— or her stupid girlfriend—to see me!" He stomped into the kitchen and grabbed the new bottle of whiskey. After a couple of belts, he welcomed the peppery burn at the back of his throat and began to feel calm.

"I have a plan." He took another hit. "Just stick to the damn plan!"

He sat the bottle on the counter and retraced his steps back to his car. Grabbing the two bags of groceries from the back seat, he noticed a Stone County Sheriff's car passing by. Hair stood up on the back of his neck, but he relaxed when the driver never looked his way. A sack cradled in each arm, he headed back inside.

After making a couple of fried bologna sandwiches, he sat at the dinette table and proceeded to enjoy his lunch. The hog of whiskey was within reach, and he added it to the table.

It might not be a fancy mimosa, but alcohol was alcohol. Besides, whiskey was more effective.

A yellow pad lay where he'd left it this morning. He grabbed it and reread his plan for capturing Harley Harper. His biggest hurdle would be getting her away from the New York bitch at the Rocky River Bar's Christmas Eve party. If he'd correctly sized up the blonde bombshell, though, he knew she'd want to keep the champagne flowing. All he'd have to do would be to spike Harley's glass, then snatching her would be easy.

He wouldn't have much time, but if he made it to his newly-discovered cabin outside of Stoneybrook, he would have all night with Harley to unwrap his present. He planned to thoroughly enjoy his gift before placing the spoiled package under the majestic, decorated Douglas fir tree in front of City Hall on Christmas.

CHAPTER THIRTEEN

"Morning," Harley's raspy voice echoed through his phone.

"Morning," Wyatt replied, wishing she was lying next to him.

"Merry Christmas Eve Eve," she said, then giggled at his silence. "I'm guessing you never watched *Friends*?"

"No, 'fraid not." Wyatt yawned. "What are your plans for the day?"

"Busy wants to do more Christmas baking, which will require a trip to DairyMart right after coffee," Harley said. "What about you?"

"Oh, just the usual, hunting a killer." Wyatt stifled another yawn. "Any chance you'd skip shopping and stay home?"

At first, he thought the line went dead, but then he could hear Harley breathing. He knew she didn't like being bossed, but he'd be better able to focus on his investigation if he knew she was safely at home.

"I'm sorry," he said. "I ruined your jolly mood."

"No. I just feel bad for you and your deputies trying to solve a murder during the holidays." Harley's sigh almost felt like she'd breathed into his ear. "Busy and I will be fine, and I'll text you when we get home."

He could hear a muffled voice and something about coffee, followed by Harley's response, "Coming."

"I'll let you go," Wyatt said.

"Wyatt."

He loved the way his name sounded when she said it. "Yes?"

"Be careful."

"Always, Ms. Harper."

"See you tomorrow night at Claire's Christmas Eve party?"

"Maybe." He wanted to say yes. Wanted to promise to take her home so they could wake up together Christmas morning. Wanted to say … *No, not yet*, he silently reminded himself.

"Maybe's better than no," Harley said, her tone filled with hope.

"Promise you'll be careful," Wyatt said.

"I will if you will," she countered.

"Done. Go enjoy coffee with Busy and I'll talk to you later today," he said.

Their *byes* crossed each other before they disconnected. Oh, how he wanted to jump in his truck and race to the Redneck Ranch, but his day was just getting started. He wasn't sleeping well. Since sleep escaped him, he'd arrived before the others and was one pot of coffee in before seven.

He heard a key in the lock and looked up to see Derrick pushing through the doors, a blast of cold air streaming in behind him. Wyatt knew Derrick would get a cup of coffee first, then sit at his desk, checking emails and then the news wires. Next, he'd refill his cup and join Wyatt in his office.

Wyatt's phone buzzed with an incoming text.

Barnes: *Will be late. Meeting Blake who might have lead.*

Wyatt: *Copy*

"Good morning." Derrick stood in the doorway, a cup in each hand.

"Morning." Surprised by the break in his cousin's routine, Wyatt waved him in. "Anything new on your end?"

"I've located the pawn shop where Wallace bought the ring," Derrick stated as he took a seat.

"You're sure?"

"Reasonably sure, yes."

"All right." Wyatt blew on the fresh cup of coffee. "Lay it out for me."

Derrick pulled his small notepad from his shirt pocket and flipped a page. "Store is in Lebanon next to the Safeway." He read his notes for a minute. "I had called the store three times, and no one remembered a ring sale, but late last night I called again. The young woman who answered said she sold a ring to Wallace."

"Can she ID the person who pawned the ring? Did she know the ring was stolen? Are you going to meet—"

Derrick's cheeks glowed red, and he became rigid in his chair. He held up a finger but said nothing. Wyatt cursed himself for bombarding his cousin with questions. He knew better. Taking a deep breath, he leaned back in his chair to wait.

After consulting his notes for a few minutes, Derrick continued. "Fenya Petrova. She said she did not know the ring was stolen and that the man who pawned the item had a receipt." Derrick looked at Wyatt. "My guess is the receipt is fake."

Reminding himself to go slow, Wyatt asked, "Do you think she can describe him?"

Derrick looked pensive, then said, "She isn't sure but said she'd try."

"Do you have her cell number?" Wyatt reached for his phone. "I'll have Simms call her and arrange to bring her to the station."

More hesitation from Derrick, so Wyatt asked, "Would you like to go with Simms?"

A small smile and a nod, then Derrick handed Wyatt his notebook. As Wyatt dialed Simms's number, Derrick retreated to his desk. Wyatt gave Simms instructions to call Fenya and set a time to pick her up. He should tell her to bring the receipt provided by the man who pawned the ring too.

As he ended the call, Barnes and Blake entered the station. Barnes headed for his desk and Blake said good morning to Derrick, who ignored him, then ambled toward Wyatt's office. Wyatt wished, he, too, could ignore Blake.

"Morning," Blake said and leaned against the doorframe.

"What is it, Blake?" Wyatt shuffled papers on his desk.

Blake moved to the chair earlier occupied by Derrick and took a seat. "I might have a link between your murder and the serial killer I told you about."

Wyatt gave Blake his attention. "I'm listening."

"I'm not sure of his name yet, but I have a partial description and profile." Blake looked at his phone and Wyatt assumed he was checking his NOTES app.

"White male, late twenties. Approximately five-ten, a buck sixty-five." He looked up. "Drifter who works part-time jobs and never stays anywhere for very long."

"That could be a hundred different men in Stoneybrook alone, not to mention within a sixty-mile radius." Wyatt knew he sounded dismissive; however, it was hard to let bygones be bygones.

"Yep." Blake stood. "But I think it's a solid lead, so I guess I'll follow up on my own."

"Wait." Wyatt came to his feet too. "Simms and Derrick will be bringing a possible eyewitness to the station from a pawn shop in Lebanon." Wyatt looked at the door as Simms entered. "Let's have a quick meeting before they leave." He pushed past Blake and walked to the center of the room.

"Heads up, everyone," Wyatt said, and all eyes turned to him. "I know Simms and Derrick are heading to Lebanon, so I'd like to request that we all meet back here in an hour."

Blake and Barnes stood together by the chalkboard and Barnes said, "We'll write our perp's description on the board."

"Sounds good," Wyatt said, then addressed Derrick, "Try to refrain from asking this young woman too many questions on the way back from Lebanon. Understood?"

Derrick nodded and headed for the door.

"Don't worry, Chief," Simms said, his cheeks coloring when Wyatt glared at him. "It'll be fine." Keys in hand, he followed Derrick to the patrol car.

Despite asking his men to stop calling him Chief, a high school nickname he couldn't seem to shake, they continued to do so. Wyatt ran a hand through his hair. He needed some fresh air, so he retrieved his gun from his desk, grabbed his hat and keys, and headed for his truck. Hopefully, Harley was still shopping at the DairyMart. Hopefully, he could buy her a cup of coffee. Mostly, he hoped he could spend a few minutes alone with her—and steal a kiss.

CHAPTER FOURTEEN

The Rocky River Bar was decorated with Christmas Eve finery. Strands of twinkling lights crisscrossed the ceiling, dotted here and there with large red glass ornaments. The tabletops were adorned with centerpieces of clear margarita glasses filled with water, cranberries and floating candles. A large Noble fir occupied a corner next to the dance floor. It was decorated with antique ornaments reflecting the charm of Christmases long ago.

"You look mauvelous, dahling," Busy said as she picked up her champagne flute.

"Back at you." Harley toasted her bestie.

"You think I pulled this off." Busy made big circles with her hands indicating her pink, blingy western blouse, "this cowgirl look?"

"Yes." Harley smiled. "And it suits you. Have you thought anymore about moving to Stoneybrook?"

"What?" Busy coughed on her sip of champagne. "I might have been under the influence of a hot firefighter when I made that suggestion."

"But you do love it here, right?" Harley searched her friend's light blue eyes.

"It's true." Busy took a sip. "I love Stoneybrook, but mostly I love being near you."

"I know." Harley touched Busy's hand. "I broke our girl code."

"Never leave the big city!" Busy raised her flute.

Harley touched Busy's glass. "Or choose a boy over your bestie. I'm sorry I broke both rules."

"Har Har." Busy smiled at her. "If you'd married Archer, I'd be like 'damn straight' you picked a simpering boy! She drained her flute. "But Wyatt isn't a boy."

"He is quite—manly." Harley grinned.

"And romantic." Busy took a sip. "He tracked you down for a kiss." She winked at Harley.

Harley blushed and drank some mimosa.

"And …" Busy raised her glass. "I believe you just asked me to move to Stoneybrook to be closer to you, so that covers the first rule."

"It's worth consideration." Harley smiled at Busy who burst into giggles.

Their laughter bounced off the walls of the almost-empty Rocky River Bar. Claire heard them and sauntered over.

"What's so funny?" She sat next to Harley.

"Busy's moving to Oregon to help me with the Redneck Ranch," Harley said.

"Oh, my stars, I would've never guessed that." Claire signaled a waiter, indicating another round.

"Har Har!" Busy gasped. "You know I'm not a country girl. How would I live without the city, or shopping, or champagne?"

"Oh, girlfriend, I can order as much champagne as you need." Claire touched Busy's arm. "And you can learn to be a country girl. Besides, we'd love to have you join us here in Stoneybrook."

Busy gave Harley a wide-eyed stare, but said to Claire, "You're too kind, dahling. I guess it can't hurt to think about it."

"Great!" Claire stood when a new group of guests arrived. "Enjoy the prime rib and the potato bar. The truffle fries are my favorite. I'll check on you in a few."

"Thanks, Claire," Harley said as the bar owner dashed off.

"You could at least come stay with me for the summer and see if you like small town life," Harley said as Dyani Belle delivered two more glasses of champagne.

"Heard you're finally giving up the big city and moving here," Dyani said, winking at Harley.

Narrowing her eyes and lifting her glass, Busy said, "Maybe." She took a sip. "How hot is it here in the summer?"

"Hot enough to head to the river every damn day." Dyani smiled and headed back to the bar.

Harley shrugged. "It's tolerable, but not as nice as The Hamptons."

"As in we'll need a pool?" Busy grinned. "Cause I don't think I can swim in a river."

"Sure." Harley took another sip. "An above-ground pool."

"Deal!" Busy clinked Harley's glass. "I'll be here the first of June."

Harley saw Ace before Busy did. She tried not to let the shock of seeing him with a date register on her face.

"We should go get some food." Harley took a sip of champagne and stood.

"What's going on?" Busy swiveled her head, then looked back at Harley. "Well, shit."

"Harley. Busy." Ace stopped at their table. "It's good to see you both."

"Nice to see you too, Ace." Harley was somewhat relieved that Ace's date had made a beeline for the bar.

Busy followed her lead, smiled, and said, "Yes, it's great to see you."

Ace looked over his shoulder, then back at them. "How long are you visiting?" he asked Busy.

"Through the new year." She took a big sip of champagne.

"Maybe we can grab coffee," Ace said, then gave a slight bow and headed toward the bar.

"Don't say it." Busy covered her face with her hands. Harley resumed her seat and waited. "I've been drooling over the smell of those truffle fries, so let's fill our plates."

"The prime rib smells amazing too." Harley sipped champagne and let her questions about Ace go for the moment. "I need to use the little girl's room first, but you can start without me if you want."

Despite a touch of sadness in her blue eyes, Busy smiled. "I'll wait for you."

As Harley headed to the back of the bar, the cacophony of sound caused her head to pound. She suddenly felt unsteady on her feet and grabbed a chair back for support. She didn't think she'd had that much champagne, although she also hadn't eaten much today. *Probably just hungry*, she told herself and continued to the bathroom.

The block letters of the word *WOMEN* printed on the door seemed to swim before her eyes. The next thing she knew someone had grabbed her arm, propelling her toward the back exit.

Harley tried to protest, but her slurred, "Let go of me," was barely audible.

"It's okay," a faceless voice said. "I'll take good care of you."

The last thing Harley remembered thinking was, *Wyatt's going to kill you.*

CHAPTER FIFTEEN

Derrick taped the sketch onto the chalkboard next to a printed list of their suspected killer's physical traits. Fenya Petrova had been very detailed in her description of the man who'd pawned the ring Wallace Dunn eventually bought. That, combined with the information Blake had discovered, seemed to confirm their assumption that Sam "Sonny" Arnold was their man.

"I know it's Christmas Eve," Wyatt said. "But we need to do our best to apprehend Arnold as soon as possible."

"It's okay, Chief," Simms said. "We want the SOB behind bars too."

Wyatt frowned at the moniker, then said, "Blake, did you chase down an address for Arnold?"

"Yep." Blake looked at his phone. "Two one seven, Twenty-fourth Street. According to the DMV, he doesn't have a driver's license.

"Derrick and I will search his house." Wyatt waved a search warrant. "I'd like you three to distribute his picture to every business throughout Stoneybrook."

"I already faxed it to the Lebanon Police Department," Barnes said. "Should I send it to the state police as well?"

Wyatt shook his head. "Not yet. Let's all meet back here …" he looked at his watch, "in an hour. If we have more solid evidence by then, we can alert the state police."

"Copy." Barnes handed stacks of the sketch to Simms and Blake.

Derrick was already out the door and Wyatt followed him to his truck. Wyatt remained silent as he drove through the quiet streets of Stoneybrook. He knew his cousin would use the downtime in the truck to process all the information they'd learned through his computer-like mind.

Wyatt swung his truck into a weed-choked driveway. They stepped out and trudged through an unkempt front yard, up a couple of stairs, then Wyatt knocked on the front door. No answer. He tested the doorknob. It wasn't locked, so he stepped inside and called, "Stone County Sheriff's Department."

His words echoed through the empty dwelling as Derrick began his methodical search. The house was small, so their initial search took about twenty-five minutes and turned up nothing useful.

"What do you think?" Wyatt asked Derrick.

Derrick didn't answer, his eyes darting from one spot to another. Tilting his head, he stared at a grubby fireplace. He crossed the small living room, dodging debris littered across the floor, and ran his fingertips across a few bricks. He stopped and began to pry a loose brick free with his pocketknife. Once he'd removed the piece, Derrick reached in and retrieved a small black bag. He turned and faced Wyatt, a knowing smile on his face.

Derrick loosened the strings, then poured four rings into his hand. "We have him now," Derrick declared.

"Good work, cousin." Wyatt gave him a soft tap on the shoulder. "Let's get these back to the station."

Wyatt's cell rang and Blake's name showed on the screen. He answered with, "What?"

"You need to come to the Rocky River Bar." Blake paused, then said. "Harley's been kidnapped."

"Harley's been taken from Rocky River." Wyatt bolted for his truck. "Derrick!" he yelled as he cranked the engine.

Derrick jumped into the passenger seat and showed Wyatt a framed photo.

"Look familiar?" Derrick asked.

Wyatt nodded, backed out, and jammed the lever into drive. He pushed down the accelerator. Tires squealing, he headed for the forest outside of Stoneybrook.

Derrick had recognized the shack in the picture. It had belonged to Carl Yates, a killer who'd finally met his demise at the hands of Sylvie Owen last June.

CHAPTER SIXTEEN

God her head hurt. Harley opened her eyes, and then panic set in. She was lying on a dirty mattress in a canopy-covered pickup bed. The memory of how she got there flooded her brain.

A man she didn't know took her from the Rocky River Bar. She'd tried to break away from him but had felt weighed down and foggy-headed. She remembered him talking to her as if she was his girlfriend. Calling her baby and saying she'd feel better when they got home. The last thing she saw before passing out was a pair of cold, dark eyes hovering above a maniacal grin.

Harley lay still and listened. She could hear him singing badly to a song she didn't know. She moved her arms and legs, surprised she hadn't been restrained. If she was going to escape, Harley knew she'd need to position herself up against the tailgate and lift the canopy door—all without alerting her captor.

After a silent prayer and a deep breath, Harley inched her way to the back of the pickup bed. She groped around until she found the handle. Bile crawled up her throat when it occurred to her that the door might be locked. That would explain why she wasn't tied up. She bit her lip and turned the handle, relieved when it opened.

Harley pushed the door slightly, knowing the hydraulics would lift it all the way with little effort. From the bumping and jerking, she assumed they were driving down a rutted dirt road. And though they weren't moving very fast, she worried about tumbling out of the truck and being injured. Maybe she should wait for him to slow down. The decision was made for her when he slammed on the brakes and yelled, "What the hell are ya doin'?"

Harley shoved the canopy door, swung a leg over the tailgate, and jumped. It wasn't graceful, but she managed to tuck and roll, then spring to her feet. She didn't know what she'd hurt, except that pain shot through her as she bolted for the trees lining the road. An almost full moon helped her adjust to the darkness. She could hear her abductor crashing through the underbrush behind her, but she didn't slow down. If he was going to kill her, or God knows what else, she planned to put up a fight.

"Go ahead and run, bitch!" he called behind her. "I love a good chase!"

Harley's lungs burned and she worried she couldn't keep up the pace. What had Wyatt said about being chased? *At the first opportunity, change your course and double back.* Great advice, but he'd never shown her how to do such a thing. The bright moon overhead guided her, and she could tell the forest was thinning out in front of her. She'd have to make a move soon or he'd be able to see her in the open.

Harley began to gradually run to the right, straining to hear if the kidnapper was still in pursuit. She'd made a good decision. The trees were suddenly larger and thicker now. Harley hoped the denseness of the wooded area would hide her because she had to slow down to dodge the massive Douglas firs surrounding her.

She'd just stepped around a large tree when a shot rang out. "Shit!" Harley cried, and began running despite the obstacles in her way.

"When I catch ya, bitch." Another bang from his gun. "I'm gonna enjoy making ya pay."

Tears streamed down Harley's cheeks and her legs felt like they would crumple beneath her. She'd rather die than be captured. Maybe she should just stop and let him shoot her. Or, maybe she should take a stand and use the defense techniques she'd learned in the classes Wyatt had paid for a few months ago.

Harley stumbled and fell over a decaying log. Before she could get to her feet, she heard him closing the distance between them. She blindly reached out in search of a weapon, her hand finally landing on a chunk of wood. When he got close enough, she would hit him with the club. If he went down, she'd proceed to beat him to death.

"I can smell your perfume, girlie," he called to her. "Come on out and we'll have ourselves a lil' fun."

Harley wrinkled her nose when his stench reached her. She gripped her stick and peeked over the log. He had his back to her, and she decided to make her move. Jumping to her feet, she swung the tree limb with all her might and connected with the back of his head.

"Bitch!" he shouted as he whirled around and lunged at her. Harley leapt out of the way and swung the club again, catching him on the arm.

"Fuck!" He dove at her, and they went down in a heap. "I'm gonna do things to ya, ya never heard of."

Harley flailed at him, but he managed to pin her arms over her head with one hand. "No! Stop!" she pleaded.

"Cry all ya want, cain't no one hear ya," he said as he ripped her blouse open with his free hand.

Harley bit the arm holding her down and he howled. "That's it, fight me!" He backhanded her across the face, splitting her lip open. "I love me a good fight."

Ears ringing, Harley closed her eyes in an effort to keep from vomiting. He grabbed her chin and shook her head. "Look at me bitch!" She glared at him. "I want ya to see how a real man enjoys himself."

He grabbed her breast, then ran his hand down her abdomen and began unbuttoning her Wranglers.

Harley kicked her legs and tried to push him off of her, but she couldn't dislodge him.

"I wanted to take my time, but ya got me all wound up with our lil' chase and wrasslin', so I'm gonna have to have ya right now." He began shoving her jeans down, and Harley closed her eyes again as tears silently rolled off her face.

A loud crack reverberated through the forest and her rapist fell forward, landing on top of her. Blood oozed from his chest. Harley scrambled from beneath him and crawled away. Pulling her jeans up, she searched the foliage but didn't see anything. Then she saw flashlights and heard Wyatt calling her name.

"I'm here," she said, struggling to her feet. "Over here."

Wyatt hurried to her, wrapped her in his coat, and held her in his arms. "I'm taking her home," he said to Barnes.

Harley looked around to see Barnes, Simms, Blake, and Derrick arched around the dead man.

"Copy," Barnes said. "We'll take care of the scene."

"Document everything," Wyatt instructed as he guided Harley toward the road.

"Copy," Derrick said. "We'll make sure no one questions the shooting."

"Find out who owns the cabin." Wyatt said over his shoulder. "If there's no current owner, have the place demolished."

Without another word, Harley and Wyatt lumbered from the woods. She leaned into him, and he held her tighter.

When they reached his truck, he helped her inside, then kissed her. His mustache coarse against her cut, bruised lip.

"Thank—" Harley swallowed a sob. "Thank you for the self-defense classes."

"I love you, Harley," he replied, and then held her as she cried.

CHAPTER SEVENTEEN

Buckeye, her crowing hen began her Christmas morning serenade at seven, two hours later than her usual summer wake-up call. Harley rolled over to find the space next to her empty and for a second, panicked.

Her ordeal last night had been taxing. She still felt shaken after almost being raped and murdered at the hands of Sonny Arnold. Thankfully, just like the end of a romantic thriller, her cowboy had come to her rescue.

Credit for saving her belonged to the whole sheriff's department, along with Busy, who'd alerted them to Harley's abduction. But the true hero was Derrick—and his photographic memory. He'd recognized a picture on the fireplace mantel in Sonny's rented house of the rundown cabin he'd found in the woods. Derrick remembered the cabin had once belonged to Carl Yates and they knew exactly where it was located.

They'd raced into the woods toward the old cabin, discovering the abandoned pickup truck. Wyatt, the deputies, and Blake rushed into the woods to search for Harley. The report from Wyatt's rifle rang in her ears as the memory of her last terrifying moments with Arnold jerked through her mind like a bad B movie.

"I will not let him steal one more minute from me," Harley vowed as she eased out of bed. She allowed Wyatt's, 'I love you' to replace the horrific memory. She checked her swollen elbow and cut lip in the mirror above her dresser as she replayed Wyatt's tender care after they'd returned to the Redneck Ranch. He'd assisted her shower, then applied salve to her various cuts, and helped her dress in sweats and a long-sleeved shirt.

Now, as she released her long locks from the hair tie, coffee wafted up the staircase as she descended to the kitchen. Wyatt and Busy sat at the dinette table enjoying the cinnamon rolls Harley and Busy had stayed up late making while Wyatt had watched. Harley knew sleep would elude them all, and the ritual of baking had been the perfect elixir.

Wyatt came to his feet and crossed to her in long strides. He gently kissed her bruised and cut lips, then said, "Merry Christmas."

Busy jumped up and poured Harley a cup of coffee. "Come sit with us. We're planning the menu for today's feast."

Harley smiled at her bestie, who looked like an older version of Cindy-Loo Who, wrapped in a fuzzy, pink bathrobe. Harley took a seat next to Wyatt, who placed a hand on her knee.

"So." Busy slid a notepad across the table to Harley. "We're thinking prime rib with all the fixings for Christmas dinner. If it's okay, I thought I'd assign each guest a dish to bring."

Harley looked at the guest list, which included the assigned menu items. Hannah and Luke were to bring a green salad. Chet Barnes and Pete Simms, who would probably bring their girlfriends too, were in charge of a charcuterie board. Blake was assigned garlic mashed potatoes. Derrick would bring his favorite BBQ chips and Echo would make her delicious homemade ranch dip. They'd requested rolls and pecan pie from Mercy and champagne for mimosas from Claire. Britt had been assigned beer and Ella was bringing hot spiced wine. Dyani planned to bring a traditional Native American Christmas cake.

"It sounds perfect," Harley said to Busy, then to Wyatt, "And I'm assuming you're in charge of the prime rib, so what's my dish?"

"Oh, that's easy," Busy said. "You're in charge of the holiday spirit. You know, greeting everyone, handing out all the gifts I know you've stashed somewhere, and simply enjoying yourself."

Tears sprang to Harley's eyes. "Thanks, Busy. I think I can manage that."

"All right, now that it's settled, give me your phone. I'll text everyone to say we're on for dinner at two."

Harley handed over her phone as Busy kissed her on the cheek. "You know," Busy said. "I might have to move to Stoneybrook sooner than later." And then she dashed off to finish her planning.

Wyatt stood, pulled Harley to her feet, and tenderly kissed her again. When he finally released her lips, she was breathless and thinking how lucky she was to have him in her life.

"Having you here, safe in my arms," his voice grew thick, "is the best Christmas gift a guy could ask for."

Harley stood on tiptoes and bussed his lips. "I love you too, Wyatt."

~ MERRY CHRISTMAS ~

ACKNOWLEDGEMENTS

Though heartfelt, my simple "thank you" seems lacking when acknowledging my team of editors: Sharon North, Story Editor, Joyce Wise, Editor. These women dedicated endless hours and offered excellent suggestions to help **FIVE GOLDEN RINGS** become a mysterious Christmas story. Their combined eye for detail has made me a better writer. I'd also like to thank my Beta Readers, Stacy Robinson, Mary Eastman, and Cindy Schmid who bolstered my confidence with kind words of praise.

DISCLOSURES

My team of editors and readers, including myself, made every effort to ensure this novel is error free. But we're human, so please accept our apologies for any mistakes you may find. Should you uncover errors while enjoying **FIVE GOLDEN RINGS**, please feel free to email me at: author.kimilakay.com

ABOUT THE AUTHOR

Kimila Kay lives in Donald, Oregon with her husband, Randy, and a feisty black cat, Halle.

She is currently a member of Northwest Independent Writers Association (NIWA), Ladies of Mystery, Sisters in Crime, Willamette Writers, and Windtree Press.

Five Golden Rings is the second novel in the Stoneybrook Mysteries series. Redneck Ranch, Book One, is also available on Amazon. Whispering Willows, Novella/Book Three and Willows Woods, Book Four, will both be available in 2024.

Her cross-cultural series, Mexico Mayhem, includes Peril in Paradise and Malice in Mazatlán. Vanished in Vallarta is now available on Amazon. Still planned for the series are Chaos in Cabo (2024), Lost in Loreto, and Fiasco in Peñasco.

You can learn more about Kimila through her blog posts on her website, Ladies of Mystery, and Windtree Press.

WHISPERING WILLOWS

KIMILA KAY

The truth whispered through the weeping willows. An echo undiscernible to the human ear, but the truth, nonetheless. An unimaginable reveal regarding the disappearance of Willow Atwood. Just listen … listen to the whispering weeping willows.

CHAPTER ONE

Echo stared at the screen but didn't react to the news.

Wyatt knew the young woman rarely spoke and never about the disappearance of her sister Willow. She touched the laptop screen with a finger then looked at him, tears in her light gray eyes. The monitor showed a picture of a tattered pink T-shirt featuring a brown bear holding a bouquet of daisies. It was the shirt their mom remembered Willow wearing the day she disappeared.

"Since it's Saturday, we won't know the identity of the remains for a few days." Wyatt hoped if he approached her in a calm manner Echo would be able to discuss the awful day her sister went missing. "It would help if we had your DNA for comparison." His knee bumped Echo's when he turned to look at Derrick, standing at the ready with a buccal swab.

"Open your mouth wide." Derrick stepped closer to Echo. "And I'll swab your cheek."

Echo looked at Derrick, then Wyatt. Nodding at Derrick, she parted her lips. A hint of tuna drifted on her breath.

Derrick angled the swab toward Echo, who leaned back, her eyes round and wary.

"Say ah," Derrick instructed. When she complied, he inserted the long swab and did a quick circle against her cheek, then slid the collection tool into a paper sleeve.

"I'll prepare this for the crime lab." Derrick walked to his desk.

Echo wiped her lips with the back of her hand and looked at the computer screen again.

"Do you know if Willow had any broken bones?" Wyatt asked.

"No." Echo tilted her head. "I mean, I don't remember." Tears trickled down her cheeks.

Wyatt handed her a tissue box as Derrick joined them.

"Willow fell from her bike." Derrick looked at Echo as if he expected her to agree.

"How old was she?" Wyatt reached for his notepad and a pen.

"I don't …" Echo began, then shrugged.

"It was before the trip into the woods," Derrick stated. "She would have been thir—"

Echo drew her knees to her chest and began rocking back and forth in her chair. She stared straight ahead, and Wyatt knew she didn't see what was in front of her. But what had happened to her, Willow, and their friend Leah five years ago.

Wyatt looked at Derrick and worried Echo wouldn't be the only one having a meltdown in the Sheriff's station.

"Derrick." Wyatt spoke softly. "Take your seat."

Derrick nodded and moved to his desk. Wyatt placed a hand on Echo's arm. He wasn't sure if soothing her was like helping his autistic cousin, but he didn't know what else to try.

Wyatt heard Derrick crack open his usual go-to, a Diet Coke, followed by pencil scratches on paper, and knew his cousin was writing in one of his notebooks. Wyatt sipped cold coffee and waited.

Echo continued to rock but made no sound and still stared ahead. Derrick's dad, Sheriff Austin Stone, had originally assigned Wyatt and Derrick to work the incident. Blake, Wyatt's brother also joined them on the case. Wyatt wished he didn't need to review the tragic events, but his mind had already headed back in time.

News of the missing girls had reached them when Leah's hysterical mom burst into the station.

"Sheriff Stone!" Vada Keller looked around the lobby. "My Leah and her friends are missing at Willow Lake. Lara Evans dropped the girls off, then went to see her boyfriend. When she came back for them, they weren't waiting in the parking lot. I-I'm worried."

"The Sheriff is out right now, but we can help." Blake moved a chair close to Vada. "Here, have a seat."

"No, no," She shook her head, "it's going to be dark soon …"

"Do you know where they were at the lake?" Wyatt picked up his phone and started a group text to the other deputies.

"They liked to go to the willow grove for a picnic." Vada ran a hand through her unkempt hair. "I told Leah to be sure and catch a ride back with Lara." Concern accentuated the fine lines around her eyes. "It isn't safe to be there after dark."

"We'll find them, Mrs. Keller." Blake escorted her toward the door. "We need you to go home in case the girls show up at your house."

A sobbing Vada Keller left, and the sheriff's department went to work. They searched the woods until it was too dark to see—even with flashlights. The next morning Wyatt and his men were joined by Fire Chief Marcus Brennan and a few of his firefighters.

When the setting sun painted the tips of the trees orange, Wyatt worried they would have to call it a night again without finding the girls.

"Here!" Ace, one of the firefighters, had shouted. "I found Cedar!"

The search party circled the girl, who lie unconscious, but breathing. Mac enlisted his men to stabilize Cedar on the picnic blanket and radioed the ambulance parked at the lodge.

"The EMTs are on their way," Mac told Wyatt. "We'll carry her toward them," he said as his men lifted the blanket and headed for the trail.

"Keep me posted on her condition," Wyatt called after Mac.

"Copy." Mac gave a wave and followed his crew.

"Wyatt," Derrick said behind him.

"What?" He knew from the look on Derrick's face the news wasn't good.

"I found Leah." Derrick turned and walked toward a patch of daisies.

Wyatt followed his cousin to where the young girl's body lay. She was partially clothed, and Wyatt could tell her last minutes with her killer had been awful. He wanted to cover Leah to give her some dignity, but he knew that would contaminate the scene.

Derrick was already on the phone with the coroner's office. Next, he'd request the Oregon state police and Crime Scene Unit from Salem.

"Wyatt." Deputy Simms approached, carrying a backpack. "I found this next to the picnic area." He lifted the pack. "Willow's name is printed on the inside. And …" He pointed to blood on the strap.

Wyatt was jolted out of the memory when Echo shot to her feet and ran from the station.

He started to follow her, but Derrick stopped him. "Let her go. She needs to process the possibility we've found Willow's remains. Trying to talk to her will extend her shutdown."

Wyatt nodded and watched as Cedar Atwood ran down Main Street on her way back to her small house near the Babbling Brook Café.

The only girl rescued from the willow grove, Cedar, was questioned several times as they tried to piece together what had happened. Other than saying their attacker had been a boy, her only response to anything they asked was to repeat the question.

Her speech pattern had remained the same over the years, earning her the nickname Echo.

CHAPTER TWO

Harley let Elvis have the round pen all to himself as she organized the tack along the fence line, then shoveled manure into a wheelbarrow. The ginormous quarter horse followed her around like a big black dragon, curious about everything she was doing. The ten-year-old, seventeen hand Elvis was an anomaly when it came to his size. Despite his massive build, he reminded Harley of a big teenager.

Wyatt was coming to dinner, so Harley wanted to finish her long list of Saturday chores. Then she'd have an hour to get ready for their evening. Mid-May had brought warm days with cool evenings. Tonight's weather would be perfect for barbequing the T-Bones Wyatt planned to grill. She could almost taste the summer salad she had decided to make as a side dish.

As she finished rolling the hose after watering down the round pen, Harley thought about her first year as the owner of the Redneck Ranch.

She and the ranch had survived a raging fire thanks to help from Wyatt and the residents of Stoneybrook. They had originally given her the nickname *greenhorn*, but now welcomed her into the fold. Stoneybrook had seen three young women murdered over the span of seven years, but the mystery had been solved not long after Harley arrived in Stoneybrook. And now she was no longer afraid of her ancient barn where two of the bodies had been found. After her rescue from a serial killer during Christmastime, Harley and Wyatt had grown closer, finally sharing their first "I love yous."

Now, as she finished up her chores, she marveled at how uneventful the first five months of this year had been. She loved her life in Stoneybrook. Smiling, she realized, besides her mom and younger brother Harrison, the only thing she missed about New York was her bestie, Busy, who was planning a visit next week.

Elvis whinnied from the round pen, where she'd left him while cleaning his stall. After she'd acquired the gigantic horse, Wyatt had helped her expand Elvis's stall and he now had access to a small outside area. Wyatt kept encouraging Harley to ride her new horse, but she didn't think her riding skills were honed enough to manage Elvis.

Wiping sweat from her brow, she did a slow turn to make sure she hadn't forgotten to feed someone or fill their water buckets. The minis, Scarlett and Rhett, were munching hay, and Hoss, her old hog, snuffled the ground looking for scraps he'd knocked out of his dish. Pigmy goat siblings Butch and

Sundance, had darted outside and found a sunny patch of grass to munch.

Her other equine charges, Maverick and Trigger, tugged hay from their feed bags, both stepping to their gates for a drive-by pet as she walked toward the round pen.

"Okay, big guy," she took Elvis by the halter, "your suite is all clean and dinner has been served."

Harley heard Buckeye and the other chickens squawking, which meant Trampas was playing his nightly game of chase. She tucked Elvis into his stall and smiled when he sniffed the fresh pine shavings. Harley held her hand up and waited for him to say goodnight. The monster horse centered the star on his forehead against her palm.

"Goodnight, Elvis." Harley removed his halter and rubbed his face until he stepped away, heading for his feed bag.

She turned off the big overhead lights, then flicked the switch for the dimmer bulbs and exited the barn. As she made her way to the stairs leading to the wraparound porch of her old farmhouse, Harley smiled at Miss Kitty and Festus, both enjoying the large cat condo she'd set up for them.

After stepping into the mudroom, she shucked her boots and grabbed a bottle of water from the fridge, then headed upstairs for a much-needed shower. First, she double-checked her outfit for the evening. Her aqua sundress paired perfectly with the new turquoise dragonfly necklace, a gift from Wyatt for her one-year anniversary at the Redneck Ranch.

Her phone chimed before she stepped into the shower, and she smiled at Busy's text.

Busy: *Changed flight to arrive tomorrow. Land Eugene at three. I'll take Uber.*

Good thing Elizabeth Benton came from money, because an Uber ride to Stoneybrook would cost her a bundle.

CHAPTER THREE

You didn't bury the bones deep enough!" his mother yelled at him.

"It was three years ago." He gave her a blank stare.

"Well, I'm guessin' with all the new-fangled DNA tests they might figure out who she is and what you did to her before—"

Her words trailed off when he came to his feet.

"I told you we shouldn't have come back here to the gulch. No telling what evidence we've left in the damn woods."

A young woman, trailed by a small child, entered the kitchen and her smile faded when he looked at her.

"I … I thought I'd start dinner."

He stepped toward her and kissed her, ignoring her recoil. The little girl grinned at him, but he didn't acknowledge her except to say, "She's filthy, give her a bath."

The young woman tucked the child behind her and muttered, "After dinner."

He headed for the door, but the old woman's nagging brought him to a halt.

"You cain't bring another girl here, not after she let the last one escape." She glared at the young woman. "It's your job to watch the girls, you dumb bitch." She yelled, spittle flying through the air.

Suppressing a smile when the young woman squared off against his mother, he barked, "Leave her alone."

She whipped around, her hand held high and ready to slap him. "Don't talk to your mother that way."

He grabbed her wrist before she could strike him, the stale odor of cigarette smoke and cheap whiskey emanating from her.

The young woman stepped back, shielding the child.

"I'll talk to you any way I want, *mother*," he growled.

He grabbed a generic beer from the fridge. Glancing at the young woman before he stalked from the rundown hovel, he said, "Come get me when my dinner is ready."

He banged through the screen door and headed for the shed he'd converted into a holding room. A tinge of anger spiked his heart rate when he thought about arriving at their previous dwelling and finding everything burned to the ground. Luckily for him, the gullies and ravines were filled with deserted buildings. This rundown collection had the perfect sized shed and a bigger shack with a kitchen. Someone had also dug a well which was a bonus. He'd been lucky to find a used 10,000-watt generator, so they had plenty of power for the ramshackle house.

Still, he thought they would've been better off staying in northern California. They hadn't yet left any bodies in the Shasta National Forest, and they had managed to move from one small town to another without drawing any attention.

His anger peaked when he thought about his mother. She was actually to blame for the girl's death. Before he could touch the girl, his mother had backhanded the kid when she wouldn't eat leftover meatloaf. The girl had fallen from her chair and hit her head on the edge of the cabinets. She wouldn't stop crying, so his mother insisted he put her in the shed. He found the young captive dead the next morning. Of course, he knew ultimately if he hadn't kidnapped her, his mother couldn't have delivered the blow that killed the young girl. And now the remains had been found.

God, how he hated his mother. All she'd ever done was make him feel inadequate. When puberty hit, she'd made him feel like a pervert for kissing a local girl. He'd tried to explain it wasn't his idea to hide in the garden shed in the girl's backyard. That he hadn't forced her to take off her clothes. Or asked her to touch him. It didn't matter what he told his mother. She'd beat him within an inch of his life, then packed up their miserable belongings and left town.

Desire, colored with shame, washed over him when he thought about the day he'd found the three girls in the willow grove. He hadn't meant to kill the first girl, but she wouldn't quit screaming. One of the friends sat crying and rocking back and forth. When he'd approached her; she jumped to her feet and ran. As he chased her down, the third friend rushed him with a big stick in her hand. The three of them had gone down in a heap and the crying girl hit her head, falling silent.

The friend with the stick struck him across the back and they fought until he gained control of her weapon. For the first time since he'd been taking advantage of young girls, he felt something other than rage. He felt respect and he knew he needed to keep the wild girl for himself.

His mother's recent berating had created a longing for someone new to enjoy, even though the last time had ended with the young woman freeing his newest captive. But he couldn't subdue the longing to take another girl.

As he sipped his beer, he thought about the young woman, a burning in his groin indicating he still enjoyed discovering new things about her. She was older now and even more beautiful than when he'd captured her. And despite fighting him every time he took her, they'd found a kind of balance. Not even the arrival of the child had deterred his desire for the girl he'd snatched from the woods five years ago.

But the evil animal living inside of him wanted a new challenge to feed his compulsion.

CHAPTER FOUR

After leaving his office for the day, Wyatt couldn't shake the image of Cedar Atwood bolting from the Sheriff's Station. And though Derrick had made it clear Wyatt shouldn't follow Echo, he worried about her. She had no one to talk to about the recently-discovered bones that might belong to her missing older sister, Willow.

Unlike the Kellers who'd moved away after their daughter Leah's murder, the Atwoods had stayed in Stoneybrook. Her parents waited for Echo to graduate high school, then decided to move to Nevada. Despite their best efforts, and with no explanation, their youngest daughter refused to make the move. Wyatt assumed Echo couldn't leave Stoneybrook until she knew what had happened to Willow.

Before Wyatt left, he asked Derrick again if he knew whether Willow had broken any bones. Although Derrick remembered her bike accident, he didn't recall her being injured, which meant she probably wasn't seen by a doctor.

Wyatt would have to wait for the remains to be examined to find out about any abnormalities or damage prior to the individual's death.

As he made the turn onto the highway, he thought again about the young couple who had discovered the bones while on a hike near Willow Lake. He knew Marie Davis had moved back to Stoneybrook eight months ago with her boyfriend. The couple had bought the bait and tackle shop on the highway leading to the lake. Even though the lake's resort had been shut down, there were plenty of rivers and tributaries perfect for trout fishing, so the small shop did a steady business. He made a mental note to ask Derrick if he knew the route the couple had taken on their hike.

Making the turn onto Little Creek Road, his mind jumped to the situation that had introduced him to the beautiful owner of the Redneck Ranch. Their initial encounter had occurred thanks to her errant donkey, Maverick, escaping his stall and heading for Wyatt's ranch. Then Harley's ex-fiancé found a young woman's body on the floor of her old barn. Wyatt and his deputies conducted an investigation which led them to Carl Yates, the serial killer who had terrorized Stoneybrook for seven years. Wyatt was glad the demented murderer had met his demise at the hand of his last victim, Sylvie Owen.

He pulled into Harley's driveway and parked in front of the ancient barn. The old girl looked more inviting after the facelift his high school friend, Britt Hanson, had given the barn. Lifting the butcher bag and wine carrier from Fenya's shop, he climbed out of his truck. He was glad Ms. Petrova, who'd been instrumental in helping locate the man who'd murdered Stoneybrook's resident Santa last Christmas, had made the move to town. As he did with all the local businesses, Wyatt tried to support her store as much as possible.

The afternoon air was still warm, but he could tell the night would bring cooler temperatures. *Perfect for a fire.* He climbed the stairs to the wraparound porch and used the toe of his boot to open the screen door.

"Hi." Harley greeted him with a kiss, taking the sack with their steaks.

"Hi." Wyatt hung his hat on the rack, then followed her from the mudroom. He wondered again why he'd been blessed to have this beguiling woman in his life.

He placed the wine bag onto the kitchen counter and pulled her close for a proper hello. As he kissed her, she twined her arms around his neck and leaned into him, causing him to question whether dinner was necessary.

Harley palmed his chest and smiled at him. "Do you want a beer or a glass of wine?"

He pointed to her glass sitting next to the sink. "Beer."

"It's the new blonde ale, Sunrise Surfer, from Pelican Brewery." She padded to the fridge and pulled out a cold one. "I love that it tastes like summer."

"I love how pretty you look." He took the beer in one hand and twirled her with the other. Her sundress billowed around her legs and the fresh scent of jasmine wafted over him.

Giggling, she took a breath, then said, "Why thank you, Sheriff Stone." She opened a cupboard. "Want a glass?"

"No, thanks." He popped the top and took a long drink. "Want to sit outside for a bit before we start the steaks?"

"Yes." Harley bussed his lips, picked up her glass, and led the way through the dining room to the front porch. "How was your day?" She sat in a white wicker chair.

Sitting in a matching chair, Wyatt took a drink. He stared east across fields, now green after a fire had destroyed the vegetation a year ago.

Harley placed a hand on his thigh but didn't press him for a response. She understood his job and had, unfortunately, been personally exposed to the dreadful nature of humankind.

"I made a green salad to go with our steaks." She smiled at him. "And I have adult root beer floats planned for dessert."

Wyatt pulled her onto his lap, so she sat straddling his legs, facing him. "Sounds like the perfect dessert to be enjoyed naked in your new pool."

Harley kissed him, then said, "I'm not sure the water's warm enough."

He caressed her ass. "Naked by the fire then."

She tilted her head. "What if someone drops by?"

"Ms. Harper." He pulled her hips toward him. "Are you trying to avoid being naked with me?"

"No." Harley laughed, and he felt the vibration of her body deep in his loins. "Maybe naked before dessert would help us work up an appetite for a sweet treat." She kissed him and pressed against his crotch.

"If you kiss me like that again, I'm going to need to work up an appetite before dinner."

Harley stood and took his hand, opening the screen door that led into the foyer.

His phone buzzed. Wyatt said a silent expletive, then pulled it from his shirt pocket and looked at Derrick's text.

Derrick: *Tracked down Willow's MRs. Nurse owed me a favor. No broken bones*

Wyatt: *Copy. At Harley's if you need anything*

Derrick: *Copy*

Wyatt wondered what Derrick could've done to garner a favor from the nurse who gave him Willow's medical records. He stepped into the foyer, navigated the dining room, and found Harley in the kitchen.

"Do you have to go?" she asked as she rinsed her beer glass.

"No." Stepping close to her and wrapping his arms around her waist, he waited until she turned to him, then kissed her.

When he released her lips, he said, "Are you starving?"

Harley wrapped her arms around his waist. "Yes, but not for dinner." She kissed him, then headed for the back door. "Lock the front door before you come up."

Wyatt grinned, walked back to the foyer, and thumbed the lock. They'd learned the hard way that well-meaning visitors didn't always knock and wait for an invitation.

He took the stairs two at a time to the landing, where Harley waited for him. They held hands and climbed upstairs to her bedroom.

"I missed you." Wyatt drew her into his arms and kissed her.

"I missed you, too." Harley twined her hands in his hair and brought his lips back to hers.

He slid the strap of her sundress off her shoulder, and she pulled at his polo. He let her tug his shirt over his head. When her sundress drifted to the floor, Wyatt sucked in a breath at the site before him. She reached for the buttons on his jeans, and he kicked off his boots. Harley slid his pants off his hips and pulled him onto the bed next to her.

Wyatt nuzzled her neck and Harley moaned, holding him to her. She reached for him, and he leaned into her caress. His desire for her was evident and she grinned when she pushed him onto his back, then straddled his hips. He thought he'd explode when her softness covered him. He placed his hands on her waist and Harley set an erotic pace. Wyatt focused on waiting until she found her pleasure first. When she cried out, he brought her lips to his and found his own joy.

Harley lay snuggled under his arm, her breath warm on his chest.

"How is it that each time with you" he stroked her hair, "feels like the first time?"

"Like when we first met," she looked up at him, "and thought we should go slow, but couldn't keep our hands off of each other."

"Exactly like that." Wyatt laughed. "I'm glad we didn't go slow."

"Me too," Harley slid her hand down his torso, "because I think the anticipation of *this* might have been too much." She raised up, found his lips, and covered him with her hand.

Wyatt rolled her onto her back and moved on top of her. He kissed her as he lowered himself to meet her arching hips. They found an easy rhythm and when he looked into her eyes, Wyatt smiled at the love he saw in their amber depths.

"I love you, Ms. Harper." His words blended with her cries of ecstasy.

CHAPTER FIVE

Waking in Wyatt's arms, Harley found him smiling at her. She blinked against the bright sunshine peeking through her bedroom curtains and kissed his bare chest.

"Morning," he said, his voice still husky with sleep.

"Morning." She raised up to kiss him.

"Waking with you in my arms is the best part of my day." Wyatt stroked her back until he reached her ass.

"Same." Harley stretched out on top of him.

"As much as I would like to have a repeat of last night's appetizers for breakfast." He kissed her. "I have to go."

Brushing sandy-colored bangs from his forehead, she touched her lips to his again. "Got somewhere better to be than here?"

"Nowhere is better than here." Wyatt rolled her onto her back and caressed a breast.

His phone buzzed and she groaned. "Someone has terrible timing."

Wyatt grabbed his phone from the nightstand. He looked at the text, then kissed her before climbing from the bed.

"It's Derrick," he said, and Harley could tell by the frown creasing his brow that, though he'd rather stay with her, something pressing needed his attention.

As Harley stood, Wyatt pulled on his jeans and reached for his shirt. She plucked the shorty pajamas she normally wore to bed from a yellow overstuffed armchair, then slipped them on.

"I'll make coffee." She lifted her phone from the nightstand, kissed him, and plodded down stairs. She was a little annoyed that her romantic breakfast had been interrupted, but she'd learned over the past year that Deputy Derrick Stone never bothered his cousin if it wasn't important.

The coffee maker finished brewing a full pot of hazelnut roast as Wyatt stepped into the kitchen. His sandy-blond hair wet from a shower, he looked handsome in a clean Stone County Sheriff's polo. Knowing the departure routine of her handsome sheriff, Harley poured coffee into a travel mug.

"Thanks." Wyatt took the mug from her. "Dinner?"

"Busy's coming today instead of next week. She lands in Eugene at three, so I'll have to plan around her arrival."

"Let me guess." Wyatt tilted his head. "She's taking an Uber from the airport."

"Yes." Harley laughed. "Can you imagine the cost?"

"Yes, which means Busy can afford to buy the three of us dinner." Wyatt grinned at her.

"Where are you off to?"

"The owners of the bait and tackle shop that discovered the bones want to meet with me. Of course, *me* means *us* in Derrick's world. They have more details to share about their discovery."

"Bones?" Harley inadvertently resorted to her hands on hips stance.

"Right." Wyatt met her questioning gaze. "I never answered your question last night about my day yesterday."

"It's okay." She held up a hand. "You don't have to share your work with me."

Wyatt stepped close to her and set the travel mug onto the counter. "Remember when we stayed at the lodge last year?"

Harley nodded, the memory of the young girl wandering in the dark along the edge of Willow Lake popping into her mind.

"The shop owners found bones near the willow grove and we're trying to determine if they belong to Willow Atwood."

"The girl who went missing over five years ago?"

"Yes." Wyatt put his hands on her arms. "I need to hear what else they have to tell us."

"Go, do your job, Sheriff," Harley bussed his lips, "because I know Echo and her parents need answers."

Wyatt wrapped her in his arms and kissed her as if he wished he could stay. "I'll text you this afternoon. Maybe we can have dinner at Rocky River to welcome Busy back to Stoneybrook."

"Good plan." Harley smiled at him.

Travel mug in hand, Wyatt headed from the kitchen. "Love you," he called as he banged through the screen door.

Harley repeated his sentiment. Since he was already on his phone, she assumed he didn't hear her. Watching through the kitchen window as he climbed into his pickup, she thought to herself, *You're a lucky girl, Harley Harper.*

After he drove away, she popped an English muffin into the toaster, poured herself a cup of coffee, then sat at the drop-leaf table. Her phone was text free for the moment. She imagined Busy hurrying through the routine of getting to her gate before texting to say she'd made her flight. On more than one occasion, Busy had been known to miss boarding by ten minutes since she had a slight time management problem.

The toaster lifted the browned muffin. Harley spread peanut butter across the top, then headed for the barn. She could hear Maverick whinnying from his stall and was thankful she wouldn't have to spend the day looking for the mischievous donkey. Of course, it helped that Wyatt's foreman, Luke Sloan, had reinforced the latch on Maverick's stall door. And another of Wyatt's ranch hands had strung hotwire along the fence line between her ranch and Broken River.

Harley inhaled the musky animal scent of the barn and greeted each member of her menagerie with a 'good morning' as she tended to them. She was glad she'd taken the extra time yesterday to clean stalls and tidy the barn. Being proactive had made today's chores go quicker.

As she headed back to the house, she plucked the rubber ducky thermometer from the pool. The water temperature was sixty-eight degrees.

"Busy will be disappointed if she can't swim in her pool," Harley told the duck before placing the yellow thermometer back into the water. The pH level was within the normal range, so all she needed was hot sunshine to warm the day and heat the pool.

Busy had insisted on paying for the installation of the above ground pool. Her bestie hoped to move to Stoneybrook at some point but wanted a pool to enjoy during her summer visits.

Crossing the patio, she checked the furniture she'd cleaned a couple of days ago. If the night provided an opportunity to swim, they could enjoy nightcaps by the fire afterward. The idea of drinks caused her thoughts to jump to jalapeño margaritas, and she ran through a mental list of ingredients.

"Oranges," Harley said as she climbed the back porch steps. She'd need to make a stop at DairyMart for oranges before she picked up Busy's champagne order from Claire at the Rocky River Bar.

She poured another cup of coffee and trekked upstairs to take a shower. Grabbing a fresh towel from the linen closet, Harley stepped into the bathroom and turned on the water.

As she stood under the hot spray, the spicy scent of the body wash she'd given Wyatt for their first anniversary enveloped her.

Gooseflesh bloomed on her skin as she thought about the previous night's pre-dinner interlude. What was it about the handsome sheriff that made her feel like they were the only two people who'd ever been in love? Several obvious reasons sprang to mind, but their shared chemistry seemed otherworldly, like something no one else had ever experienced.

Despite her struggle to understand her love for him, Harley knew Wyatt Stone had been the missing puzzle piece she needed to complete her life.

CHAPTER SIX

The early Sunday morning air carried the scent of wildflowers and freshly cut grass. He was surprised the campground was almost empty, given the warm spring weather. Maybe families were waiting for the upcoming Memorial Day weekend to go camping. It was also a dry camp located along one of the many tributaries feeding Willow Lake and not everyone was cut out for boondocking.

Roaming through the vacant sites, he loaded abandoned campfire wood into his wheelbarrow. A few people were milling about. Most of them ignored him, but a few said, "Good morning."

Over the years he'd learned to wear non-descript clothing: a plain baseball cap, and work boots with a well-worn sole. He always picked rundown campgrounds that weren't well-maintained or ones that didn't have a caretaker. This allowed him to assume the role of a maintenance worker.

When he'd left the crappy shack this morning, his mother was cooking bacon and eggs. She'd yelled at him he'd better pick a girl he could control. Ignoring her warning, he snitched a piece of greasy bacon, laughing at her attempt to swat him with a spatula.

He wondered what his life would be like if he left with the young woman and the little girl. If he abandoned the bitch who'd ruined his future and left her fending for herself. He didn't have any delusions life would be full of sunshine and roses, but maybe he wouldn't be a monster who kidnapped young girls.

Or maybe he might have been able to have a normal relationship if his mother hadn't branded him a disgusting, twisted pervert. If they hadn't roamed from one rundown hovel to another. If she hadn't killed his father and made him help cover up her crime.

He'd been so busy wandering down his shitty memory lane, he'd almost missed the girl picking wildflowers in a small clearing. Sunlight sparked the red highlights in her strawberry-blonde hair. For a moment he was reminded of the young woman he'd snatched from the willow grove all those years ago.

He wanted this girl. Needed this girl. Knew the young woman would be furious with him when he brought this young girl back to the shack she'd tried to make into a home.

www.ingramcontent.com/pod-product-compliance
Lightning Source LLC
Chambersburg PA
CBHW021556310726
48972CB00003B/840